CRAG ISLAND

Robert J. Foster

Crag Island

Copyright © 2024 by Robert J. Foster

Individual works are Copyright © 2024 by the respective author.

All rights reserved. The story in this book is the property of the respective author, in all media both physical and digital. No one, except the owner of this property, may reproduce, copy, or publish in any medium any individual story or part of this anthology without the express permission of the author of the work.

The contents of this book are fiction. Any resemblance to any actual person, place, or event is purely coincidental. Any opinions expressed by the authors are their own and do not reflect those of the editors or Robert J. Foster.

Cover design © 2024 Robert J. Foster
Cover designed by Austin Slade Perry

The woman in the white shirt adjusted her badge, assured herself it was on straight, swiped her card through the slot, and when two beeps sounded, she saw the light go from red to green and knew it was time to open the door. She entered a long hallway with white walls. Ernesto wasn't there to sign her in. Other guards would've been suspicious of this but it was only her third day of work and she didn't know the regular members of the shift yet. Nor was she suspicious of the lack of people in the hallway on her walk down to the office. There were no fellow guards or staff and no inmates either.

When she reached the main room, she stopped. At first, she didn't know why she had done so, but soon understood. Her ears had sent her a message, not about what she was hearing, but about what she had heard on previous days in the prison. On Sunday, when she'd completed the required training course, there had been chatter all throughout the room. There had even been voices of people that carried in from beyond the door. On Monday, the music of a janitor in Cellblock Three had echoed all the way down here. Now she heard none of those things. The room was strangely quiet.

She made her way across the space and scanned her I.D. badge one more time. Two beeps. Red changed to green and she was through. As she entered, she quickly observed the sign above the office door. It read **Crag Island Penitentiary, Security**.

She'd passed this door on both of her previous days, on her way to the office down the hall. A bespectacled man named Will always met her there and showed her how to run the monitors and intercom system in a cramped room with uncomfortable chairs, but he wasn't there today.

Her job was easy enough. She sat in the chair, watched the cameras, and reported anything that looked unusual, while Will sat nearby, telling her, "Don't worry about the inmate screaming. He always does that," and "A broken lightbulb is not an emergency. You don't have to report it." Will sounded perpetually bored and acted as though he had better things to do than train a newbie.

Especially a newbie who couldn't even pass the obstacle course.

Katarina walked through the security office door for the first time. It was time to meet the chief, who would, no doubt, want to know why she'd frozen when she'd seen the flashing image of the bloody old woman on the obstacle course. An image that brought up a half-formed memory: an old lady with overlong fingers and blood on her face, holding her little body down and painting her skin red. *How old had she been? Had it actually happened?*

This was the part she hated. A small needle in a plastic bag rested to her immediate right. A small smooth computerized panel was next to it. She ripped off the plastic wrapping and lifted the needle to her finger. To her left was a microphone. She leaned toward it and spoke.

"My name is Katarina Shai Anderson."

With that, she stuck the needle into the tip of her left ring finger and then dropped it into a wastebasket to rest with the heap of previously used ones. Next, she held her bleeding finger over the panel and let it drip. One drop. Two drops. A loud beep chirped, and she knew the computer inside was reading her voice coding. The blood seeped into the panel to be analyzed by an archaic system she did not understand. A moment later, the computer responded.

"Officer Anderson," announced the monotone voice of the office computer. "Access granted. Advance to the circle."

Being in the main office made her feel like a real guard, not a rookie failure consigned to watch cameras all day. She was now in the space of the people who did the hard work, the ones who didn't get scared during training.

Beyond the door was a small office, glass-walled on all sides, emphasizing the need to have eyes on everything on the premises. She took comfort from the knowledge that the glass was bullet/shatterproof, but it was the marking on the floor that made her feel most at ease. Katarina carefully stepped over the line of a circle composed entirely of salt. Its circumference contained the entire security office and once inside its perimeter, she breathed a sigh of relief. A tall man stood by the computer. He wore a dark blue uniform with a gold badge pinned above his left shirt pocket.

"Officer...Anderson," he said.

She could see him studying her badge, wondering who this new person was. His badge read: 'Michaels, Security Chief.'

"Sir" she began. "It's nice to..."

He cut her off with a swift motion of his long hand. Michaels was a gangly fellow, big-nosed, and would've been comical to look at if not for the cold seriousness in his eyes.

"Today, I want you to call me Phillip. And what is your name, please?"

She didn't know why the chief of security was alone in the office or why he wanted to know her name, but she answered all the same.

"Katarina," Phillip repeated. "I like to know the names of the people fighting alongside me."

"Sir?"

Once again, he cut her off.

"Katarina, we have a situation to deal with," said Phillip. "You're new, aren't you?"

She nodded. "Sir, if this is about the obstacle course, I can explain. One of the images jogged an old memory. I didn't even know I had it until I saw the picture of the old…"

He stepped closer and stared her down, cutting her off without a word. When she was silent, he said, "I don't care about the damn obstacle course. You could fail that thing five times, as long as you stand with me now. No one is going to sit at a desk today. I need you out there with me." When he thought she'd gotten the message, he went on. "I don't have long, but I'll explain what I know," said Phillip. "Our main security force is currently trapped in the canteen and my communications link to the mainland has been severed. There's no help coming. There's been a breakout, and you and I are the only security in a position to stop it."

Katarina unknowingly backed away. When she hip-checked a desk, she stopped.

"I think I know who orchestrated this, and if I can locate him, I might be able to find out how to stop it. You can stay here if you like. Don't leave the circle and you'll be alright." She didn't respond and he continued. "All security, save the two of us, are trapped dealing with chaos in the canteen. The goblins have blocked all the doors and aren't letting anyone in or out of there"

"Wow," Katarina said.

"There's more," said Phillip. "All of the cells in Block Four have been opened somehow. The inmates are out."

Katarina struggled to remember what she'd learned on her first day: Cellblock One was for minor offenses, Cellblock Two was mostly reserved for short-timers. and Cellblock Three was for inmates convicted of aggravated crimes. That meant Cellblock Four was…

"Maximum Security," she said.

"Yes," said Phillip. "I'm going after the leader. Well, I think he's the one who organized all of this."

"Who?"

"Inmate Nineteen."

Katarina had heard of this one. The guards regularly traded stories of Nineteen. They said he was brilliant. Murderous, but brilliant.

"This has Cedrick written all over it," said Phillip.

"The vampire," She'd heard of him on her first day. "And me, sir?"

"Remember your training if you need to use your sidearm. Aim for center mass and don't waste any bullets. Unfortunately, it will only help with a select few of the inmates. That's why I'm giving you these."

He handed her a strangely shaped knife. then dug his hand into a desk drawer and began rifling around for something. The knife had a curving blade that switch backed on itself to create a wave effect. Its hilt was bulbous and looked like pure ivory.

"It's a bone handle," he explained, as he searched in the drawer. "The blade is normal steel, but it was anointed years ago, so it should serve you well and will work against most inmates."

"Anointed in what?" she asked.

"No time to explain," Phillip replied. "Let's just say that it's enchanted and any inmate that's heard of it will know to steer clear of you."

Phillip withdrew his hand from the drawer. In it, he held a small plastic bag.

"While I'm searching for Cedrick, I need you rounding up the escapees of Block Four. Do you remember what you've been told about them?"

"Umm…yes," Katarina stammered. "I remember hearing about Thirty-Three."

Phillip nodded.

Crag Island

"People talk about Inmate Thirty-Three for good reason. Believe the hype. She's been here since this place opened and all the stories about her scare the hell out of me. I don't even know her name. Do not engage with her at all, understand? You see her, you run. She's slow, so she won't catch you."

Katarina believed him and the wild stories she'd heard on her first two days of work. She was frightened but not foolish. However, there was something else on her mind. She couldn't shake the memory of the most terrifying experience she'd had on her first day.

"And there's number...Twenty-four," she said.

"Margaret Harrow," acknowledged Phillip. "Yes, she's got quite the rap sheet. But she's not the one I'm most concerned about. What I want you to worry about is Ivan. Inmate Eighty-Four."

Katarina didn't know who that was and said so. Phillip was about to respond when there was a loud crash in the corridor.

"I've delayed too long already," rushed Phillip. "Corral anyone you can. Get them back in their cells. You are authorized to use force and you'll need to. Meet me back here in one hour."

Phillip shoved some more things into his pockets. Katarina saw him pick up a small bottle of liquid and a sharp piece of scrap iron. Lastly, he held up a long–pointed stake. He walked to the door and prepared to leave the office, then stopped as if he'd forgotten something.

"Take that with you."

He was pointing at the bag he'd taken out. It held a gray powder substance.

"...nitrate. Don't lose it. I'm out of the bullets."

She missed the first part of the sentence in a rising cacophony coming in from outside the office and tried to ask. Then he was out of the door, beyond the protection of the circle, and down the hallway to Cellblock Three, leaving her question unanswered.

What the hell is $AgNO3$? she wondered, reading the writing on the side of the bag. It was too late to ask Phillip, so Katarina stuffed the plastic bag into her front pocket. She checked her gun. Loaded. Safety On. The strange knife sounded important, so she decided to carry it in her hand as she moved to leave the office. She paused, then, with a deep breath, she stepped out of the salt circle.

***

To determine what had happened, Phillip would first have to find Cedrick. The vampire was notoriously sneaky and could be anywhere on the premises by now. Wandering the corridors would be a waste of time. Things were getting worse by the minute. He would need a plan. As he walked, a course of action came to mind. Phillip wasn't happy about it but it was his best chance of tracking down Cedrick.

In his twelve years as security chief, Crag Island had never had a breakout. Phillip Michaels had successfully subdued the ghost uprising of 2006 and personally put down the ghoul berserker that got out of its cell in 2013. He was as prepared as he could be, but it still nagged at him; he had missed something along the way. An inmate had finally outwitted him. As he walked determinedly through the hallways, he made an important decision. He would quell this rebellion just as he had all the others, then put in his resignation immediately. After twelve years of prison chaos, Phillip wanted nothing more than to spend the next twelve years living quietly with Anne and the kids. His wife's radiant smile flashed in his thoughts, but he had to push it away. There was business to attend to and he couldn't afford to get sentimental.

He would need to speak to Millie, Mollie, and Maeve. They had eyes everywhere.

Phillip reached into his shirt pocket and took out a tiny tin whistle. He played a quick tune, then put the whistle away again. He waited.

"Dear Phillip, it is. Yes, Millie?"

"Indeed, it is."

Phillip couldn't see them yet but knew he was being observed. They were toying with him, remaining invisible while letting him hear them. Typical fairies, always vying for the upper hand in any situation.

"Ladies," called Phillip. "I'd like to parlay if you don't mind."

A sunspot flashed by the left wall, then it wasn't a spot anymore. Petite wings took its place, flapping ever faster. From a short distance, one could easily mistake it for a hummingbird.

When he looked forward again, two more shapes had appeared, flapping incessantly in the air.

Millie, Mollie, and Maeve: Inmates Twenty-Six, Twenty-Seven, Twenty-Eight.

"Good day, ladies," Phillip said.

"Handsome as ever," said Mollie.

"Such sweet eyes," said Millie.

"Marvelous hair," said Mollie.

"So well-endowed," said Maeve.

Fairies are tricky. Although they are inherently nonviolent, one always must observe proper manners while speaking to them. Terrible things happen to humans who behave rudely in the presence of the little folk. Phillip always had to remind himself of this when he spoke to these ladies; Millie and Mollie were almost identical. They were the same size and both had wavy blonde hair and azure eyes. But, Millie always wore blue rags and Mollie preferred green. It was the only way he could tell the difference. Confusing one for the other could get him into a lot of trouble.

Maeve was the odd one out. As opposed to the clear-colored dragonfly wings of her friends, Maeve's wings were bright green and leafy. Her hair was red and she wore faded purple cloth that Phillip thought was an old scrap of curtain. What disturbed Phillip most was that Maeve's eyes never stopped moving, refusing to look at one point for more than a second or two.

"Ladies," said Phillip. "Flattering as you are, I came here to discuss something with you."

"Yes?" they asked in unison.

"I'd like to ask your assistance in finding Cedrick."

They all quickly flitted together to form a small huddle, glittering somehow through their prison clothes, as if they had shining scales underneath. Then Millie spoke.

"Yes, we can find where he is."

Phillip nodded. "I never doubted it. Would you be so kind as to tell me where I can find him?"

"So tall," said Mollie.

"Strong hands," said Millie.

"A hawk's nose," said Maeve.

This was what he'd expected. The ladies would never give unless they could get in return. It was time to make a deal. He would have to tread carefully. Fairies take deals seriously and Phillip didn't dare make any promises he couldn't keep.

"And if you were inclined to help me, what would you lovely stars like me to do for you?"

Phillip heard the faintest of giggles pass between the three of them.

"Open the window," said Mollie.

"Dear Mollie," said Phillip. "You know I can't do that. A choice like that is up to the warden. I'm not authorized to decide when you fly free."

"I did nothing," spat Millie.

"That man in Aberdeen disagrees with you, my dear Millie. As I understand it, he is still a goat. Your spell isn't estimated to wear off for the next three years."

Millie made a 'Humph' gesture with her tiny shoulders, wings drooping as she did so.

"And lady Maeve," said Phillip. "You knew perfectly well that brewing love potions inside British territory is illegal."

"He is still mine," said Maeve, a crooked smile on her too-wide lips.

"I am prepared to meet your needs, ladies, but only if we can deal in realities."

Inmates, Twenty-Six, Twenty-Seven, and Twenty-Eight conferred one more time, then Mollie spoke.

"Reduced sentences. Five years for each."

Phillip kept his voice soft, a teacher speaking to a precocious child. "I can only speak to the warden on your behalf. The final decision is his. I'm afraid that I don't believe he will grant as much as five years."

"Then we don't tell you anything," said Millie.

"Nothing from us for you," said Mollie.

"We will put snakes through your eyes as you slumber," said Maeve.

This was not going as he'd hoped and every moment that passed allowed Cedrick to further his plan. Phillip had no choice but to go on the offensive.

"Lady Maeve, I do not appreciate threats. You forget your manners, and you force me to be unpleasant."

Phillip reached into his pocket and pulled out the scrap of sharp iron. He held it out, in plain view of the fairies. They gasped audibly.

"Dastardly," said Mollie.

"Untrustworthy," said Millie.

Maeve stared quietly, red hair falling in the way of her piercing eyes, her silence more unsettling than the words of the others.

"I can speak to the warden. That is the most I can promise," said Phillip.

The fairies spoke to one another again for a few seconds and then separated once more.

"We accept your deal, dear Phillip," said Millie and Mollie simultaneously.

Maeve offered a barely audible, "Yes."

"Excellent," said Phillip. "Now, time is of the essence, if you would please point the way."

Millie zipped over to a window where she found a small insect crawling. She whispered to it briefly. The bug unfolded its wings and flew out of the room. Millie turned back to the room and motioned for the others to wait. One minute later, a small gray gull landed outside of the window and cawed loudly four times.

"Brother gull says Cedrick is in the warden's office," said Mollie.

Phillip bowed lowly, while keeping his eyes on Maeve.

"Thank you, my ladies," he said. "Be well."

Phillip walked down the hallway, still holding the iron tightly in his hand. He did not dare let go of it until he was well beyond the reach of the little folk. Maeve's stare had unsettled him more than he'd realized. As he made his way toward the warden's office, he knew he'd have to keep his promise of speaking to Warden Evans about the reduced sentences, while also knowing they would never be granted. The ladies would not be happy and he didn't know how they would react to the bad news. He shook it off. That was a problem for a later day. There was a more pressing task to deal with.

***

The corridors all looked the same; tall white walls and cold concrete floors. Turn after turn, Katarina held the special knife at the ready, sure that a threat was waiting around the next corner. Perhaps Phillip had been wrong and Cellblock Four wasn't crawling with inmates. There was a certain comfort in the thought they might have escaped the prison, but Katarina knew she was fooling herself. These creatures had been brought to Crag Island for one reason: No one escapes.

She heard a huffing that grew louder as she advanced down the hall. At the next intersection, Katarina stopped, knife raised, hand on her gun, took one long breath, and stepped out into the corridor as quickly as she could.

A small man in a green coat sat slumped against a wall, his hand resting limply on his stomach. She glimpsed his face for only a second before being drawn to the flowing puddle of red spreading beneath him. His breathing came in short bursts. His wide bearded face exhibited ceaseless pain.

"Are you alright?" asked Katarina.

A stupid question, but she didn't know what else to say.

The small man on the floor laughed. Then he doubled over, clutching his stomach. The laugh had hurt.

"You're the new one," he said.

Katarina nodded and knelt next to the little man. She noted a large gouge in his stomach. His hand was resting there, awash in blood. She did not feel any threat from this man, only a need to help him manage his pain, so she let go of the knife and leaned toward him.

"Yes," she said. "I'm Katarina."

There was too much blood. She took off her white security jacket and tried to block the wound, but it wasn't enough. It reddened in no time, and her blue collared shirt would do no better. Judging by the size of the puddle, he'd been there for a while. Moving him to the infirmary would most likely kill him. She wracked her mind but couldn't think of a way to save him.

"It's no use," he said. "I've lost too much already."

She looked at his face, rosy cheeks and bushy red beard. He looked kind. She didn't know the inmates could look as friendly as this. On his chest, Katarina saw a number sewn onto a small green pocket. Eleven.

"What's your name?" asked Katarina.

"Fergal," he replied.

She repeated the name quietly. As she pressed her security jacket against his wound, Katarina wondered why he was there. There was no violence in him. He didn't belong in Maximum Security.

"What happened?" she asked.

"The door popped open suddenly, so I left me cell. I found some steps, so I walked up here, looking for an exit. That's when I met Ivan."

It was clear to her now. He'd walked up from a lower level, convicted of a lesser crime.

"Big bastard. Tore me guts right out," said Fergal.

This was the second time she'd been warned of inmate Eighty-Four. All she knew now was that he was big, named Ivan, and was capable of ripping stomachs open.

"Is there anything you'd like me to do for you?" Katarina asked.

He thought for a moment.

"Don't get dead," Fergal said. "You're one of the good ones."

As she held him and tried to ease his mind, if not his pain, his body tensed. An instinctive reaction like the total stillness of a deer just before it breaks into a run for its life. Katarina couldn't see the long tangled hair covering the narrow wart-covered nose or the raggedy gown the woman behind her wore. If she had looked into the eyes of Margaret Harrow at that moment, she would have frozen, just like she did in training.

Fergal saw.

"Hello, witch!" he called.

Katarina, still crouched, spun on the balls

of her feet and looked. Margaret was only a few feet away and moving steadily closer. As the witch drew near, Katarina found that all she could do was fall backward onto her hands, and sit and stare. Petrified.

"Come here, girl," said Margaret Harrow. "Your pretty hair will make a fine shawl. Your shiny teeth shall be my newest necklace."

Margaret was impossibly thin with yellowed skin and deep-set eyes with pupils so pale they were all but invisible. She stepped clumsily forward and the wrinkles on her face immediately brought back the fear that had taken hold of Katarina on the obstacle course.

Katarina was struck once more by a memory of an old woman painting her with crimson liquid. She might have been eight years old. No, younger.

Katarina tried to speak and couldn't. The witch was stepping closer and she had no idea what to do. She remembered looking into Margaret's cell on her first day of work and seeing the witch in the midst of a ritual. Margaret had been bleeding out a live rat and dancing while it shrieked its rodent life away. The image burned into her memory and Katarina was terrified by a sudden thought. *I'm about to be the rat.*

"You wouldn't know what to do with teeth even if you had them," said Fergal.

The witch stopped and glared at him.

"Silence, foul leprechaun!" Margaret shouted.

Fergal turned his head and looked Katarina directly in the eyes. He nodded once, then turned back to the witch.

"And if you want to show off your new jewelry when you're out on the town, might I suggest having a nice shampoo first? Your hair is looking a bit worse for wear."

Margaret stepped toward him, gnashing her rotten teeth, and twiddling her bony fingers. Fergal patted Katarina's hand and whispered, "Go."

The touch on her hand snapped Katarina out of her stupor. She scooted backward and stood up, eyes on the witch the whole time.

"I'm going to…" Margaret said to Fergal.

"You're going somewhere?" the leprechaun interrupted. "Have a fine time. Send us a postcard."

He was still sitting, immobile, in an expanding puddle of his blood. Before she turned and ran down the corridor, Katarina noticed one difference from when she'd first found him. Now he was smiling.

The last words she heard from Fergal were faint, "You should know I don't kiss on a first—" After that, the only sounds he made were screams. Katarina was three corridors away by the time the screaming stopped.

Her breathing was heavier than she could ever remember. She bent over and placed her bloody hands on her knees, repeatedly reminding herself that the witch was far behind. Margaret Harrow couldn't reach her here. She wiped off the leprechaun blood on her dark trousers as best she could and decided to move on. Katarina was an avid runner, so despite her fear, she recovered quickly and stood up again. She looked around her. There was an intersection. She had no idea which way to go.

Left or right?

Going back the way she'd come was out of the question. Anything could be down those other halls. The corridors were empty white shells and there weren't any signs to guide her. She breathed deeply, closed her eyes, and listened. There was no sound coming from the corridor on her left. In the right hallway, however, there was…something.

Katarina opened her eyes and inched closer to the right. The sound was growing steadily louder. A light flickered in the far hallway and showed a dark shape rocking forward into view only to drop out of sight again. Then reappearing. Rocking backward behind the wall again. The sound was becoming clearer. She saw only the shadow.

Scruff. Scruff. Scruff.

The thing was slow and its movement unsteady. As it drew closer, Katarina could see its shadow cast on the far wall. It was humanoid, but had scraps hanging off its body, like long flapping tendrils. They swayed with each step and she knew it would reach the turn into her hallway in seconds.

"You see her, you run."

Those had been Phillip's words back in the office. He had been speaking of inmate Thirty-three, she who kills with a single touch. Katarina backed away slowly. The creature in the hallway was almost visible, its shadow clear on the wall. A hand, bony white with yellowed rotten wrappings dangling from it, came into view. Then the arm. Katarina knew this was inmate Thirty-three for sure.

She turned to run. The being rounded the corner behind her, sensing her life, wanting her vitality. In her ancient decrepit body, Inmate Thirty-three wanted nothing more than to put a hand on the spry young woman and to drain the life from her until they were equally desiccated. If she'd still had a larynx, if her voice hadn't left her along with her inner organs long ago, Thirty-Three would've croaked out the word, "Stop," but this running woman wouldn't understand her language, which was old before so many others.

The teeth snapped, the wrappings swayed, and there was always the incessant *Scruff! Scruff! Scruff!* of one dragging foot. Inside the old cloth wound around her body, there was still something skeletal. She was ancient. She was dead.

Katarina ran. She knew she didn't need to go as fast this time. Phillip had told the truth; the mummy was slow. As long as she could see it coming, it wouldn't catch her.

***

The warden's office was coming up, so Phillip drew the stake from his belt and held it aloft as he neared the entrance. It was best to be ready. The vampire was notoriously unpredictable.

One quick breath, then he stepped into the room. Behind the desk, sat a lean man in a dark gray suit jacket. His legs were crossed in front of him, displaying standard-issue prison pants. The contradiction in clothing caught Phillip's attention.

"I would've thought you'd had a better fashion sense," said Phillip.

The vampire smiled.

"I could say that I came to this office to oversee the great work my coworkers are doing." Cedrick motioned to the numerous monitors showing footage of the prison's halls and cells. "But if I'm truly being honest, I really just wanted to try on some of Warden Evans's things. There's nothing like the feel of donning a good suit, don't you think?"

"Do you confess that you did this?" asked Phillip.

The vampire's smile grew bigger and kept growing until it was disproportionately wide for the size of his face. His rows of jagged teeth were on full display, alternating white spikes pointing up and down. Stalagmites and stalactites in a dark cavern.

"I certainly did," said Cedrick. "Quite well, if I may toot my own horn a bit. You never saw this coming did you, old boy?"

"I worried, that's a big part of my job," said Phillip, "and I thought that if it ever happened you'd be behind it somehow."

"I'm flattered that you had such confidence in me."

"How'd you do it?" asked Phillip.

"Oh, a little this, a little that. It was rather simple in the end," said Cedrick.

The vampire leaned forward in the chair and Phillip tensed. He set one foot a bit behind him to brace himself and raised the stake. He knew how fast Cedrick was and wasn't taking any chances. A sitting vampire, moving across a flat surface, at a range of ten feet, can change its circumstances in no time at all. Cedrick's casual posture meant absolutely nothing, other than he hadn't decided to attack yet. He would, it was only a question of when.

"Let me tell you what a stay in this lovely hotel of yours does to one's mind, Phillip," the vampire said. "It first takes away your point of reference. Day and night are the same when you're in a box. Trust me, I know. But this place is different. I could always leave my coffin and

I knew when to do so. Here, however, time becomes all but meaningless."

"I don't care about your philosophical ramblings, Cedrick," said Phillip.

The vampire pulled his legs in a bit, a posture he could easily spring from. He stayed that way.

"Ahh, but you should care," said Cedrick. "You absolutely should. Because I eventually realized that although my perception of time had completely faltered, I still had plenty of it. Being a prisoner is nothing but having time. When you put me in your square room and left me there, you gave me all the time I could ever need. That was foolish of you because I used it to think."

Phillip gripped the stake tighter and glanced briefly toward the office window on the far wall.

"I will tell you exactly what I've done," said Cedrick. "I've misdirected you."

Cedrick stood slowly and brushed something lightly off of the suit he'd stolen from the warden's coat rack.

The vampire sprang.

Phillip was as ready as he could've been, but it didn't matter. Cedrick's speed left him no chance to counter. He was falling before he knew he'd been hit. Pain in his shoulder registered a moment before he crashed to the ground. Looking up from the floor, he couldn't see Cedrick anywhere. There would be a second attack any time now.

Phillip pushed himself through his dizziness and willed away his pain long enough to get back on his feet. Despite the hit he'd taken, he still had one thing going for him; he hadn't dropped the stake.

Vampires do not have reflections. They do, however, cast shadows. Phillip was lucid enough to look around the room in the most well-lit areas. Darkness had been the vampire's ally for centuries. Warden Evan's brightly lit office was not. The bright beam over the warden's cupboard showed a flicker of movement behind it. Phillip pretended not to notice, continued looking in other places, and listened as hard as he could. There was a faint rustle behind him.

Phillip spun and caught Cedrick on the point of impact. The two crashed together and their combined weight drove them into the far wall. They stood in a clinch, while the human jabbed his weapon outward and the vampire thrashed forward. Then the expression on Cedrick's face contorted and he pulled away. There was blood on the tip of the stake. Phillip allowed his hopes to rise, only to have them plummet immediately after he saw the damage he'd done. There was a large hole in Cedrick's upper chest.

"Oh, Phillip," said Cedrick. "There are no points for effort in this game. You missed."

The vampire darted left, then right, and as Phillip stepped toward him with the stake raised, Cedrick kicked a chair across the room. It smashed heavily into Phillip's knees, causing him to lose balance and tumble to the ground. Cedrick was on him before he knew it, grabbing the stake in Phillip's hand, wrenching it free from his grip, and tossing it across the room.

Cedrick turned back, then inched his teeth toward Phillip's neck.

The nosferatu are quick and ruthless; however, they do not possess superhuman strength. Despite there being only a few ways to kill them, much of their anatomy still follows human rules. They have the same skeletal structure.

Phillip yanked his neck back just in time to avoid a bite. The sudden movement distracted Cedrick, and Phillip used that time to grab his arm and twist it into an armbar.

Cedrick screamed for the first time in over one hundred years as he felt his elbow joint snap. The world went blindingly white, and when the pain subsided, he was able to twist away and get some distance.

Phillip stood. Hopefully, breaking Cedrick's arm would even things out a bit. Now he knew which direction his opponent's attacks would come from. Still, Phillip would've felt much better about his chances if he still had the stake in his hand. He involuntarily looked in the direction it had gone.

Cedrick smiled.

"Go for it," Cedrick said. "Let's see how fast you are."

One arm swinging limply by his side, Cedrick stood and waited. Phillip did not take the bait. A race to the stake was no contest, and he knew it. Then he remembered the vampire talking about his lost perception of time in the prison cell.

"You're an idiot," said Phillip. "You think I didn't plan for this?"

Cedrick began walking toward him, slowly, carefully. Phillip took a step back, toward the wall and the curtained window behind him.

"Let me ask you a question," said Phillip. "What time is it?"

Cedrick looked confused before he stopped walking, and his eyes shot wide open.

Phillip grabbed the window curtain and drew it upward in one swift motion. The vampire placed his hands over his eyes and leaped behind the desk. Phillip was one step behind him.

As he crouched, waiting for the searing rays of the sun to reach him in his hiding spot, Cedrick became angry with himself. How could he be foolish enough to fall for such a trap? Hadn't he planned for this to happen well before sunrise?

Silence.

The pain did not come and the signs of an imminent ray of light seeking to burn his flesh were not present. There was no heat and when he dared a peek around the far end of the desk, the room looked no lighter than before. He'd been fooled. There was no sun outside. Phillip had used the trick to get out of a potential attack, and he'd probably gone for the stake immediately afterward. It was time to make him pay for his ruse. Cedrick crouched low, preparing a leap toward the stake.

The burning did come, but not in the way Cedrick had expected. It was wet at first, then it dripped from the back of his head down onto his shoulder where it met his previous wound. He screamed in a register no human could equal. Dropping to his knees, feeling the wetness turn hot and sink into his skin, the vampire twisted his body around to look at his attacker. Phillip stood next to the desk, holding a small empty bottle. It had a gold crucifix printed on its front.

"Holy water, really?" said Cedrick.

"Worked, didn't it?" said Phillip.

The vampire stood but his legs were unreliable. Shaking. The burning in his skin was intensifying, going deeper into him. It was hard to focus, like trying to walk a straight line on a violently tilting ship. He took a step and faltered. Took another, and was no longer behind the desk.

"You know what's funny?" Cedrick said.

"What?" asked Phillip.

"This doesn't even matter," said Cedrick. "Even if you defeat me, I've already won. You never could see past me, could you, old boy? Never thought that my plan might not even involve my own escape."

This worried Phillip because he knew there was something he didn't understand. There was a layer of the vampire's plan he hadn't discovered yet. Cedrick's words passed through his mind: "*I've misdirected you.*"

"This is why I've always hated you humans. Homo sapiens never has been able to consider the importance of what it's not directly involved in. You are the most egotistical of animals, and I look forward to knowing we took such a massive bite out of your population."

"What are you saying?" asked Phillip.

Cedrick's expression became deadly serious as an almost palpable coldness filled the room. He looked Phillip straight in the eyes as he spoke.

"Approximately two hundred miles to our west is a small island. It is covered in villages, containing a total human population of ninety-eight people. By morning, those ninety-eight people will be dead. And that is only the beginning. The islands and landmasses get considerably larger from that point on. Then come the cities."

Phillip needed an answer, and yet was terrified of asking his upcoming question.

"What did you do, Cedrick?"

Cedrick cackled.

"I let him out."

Phillip stood, frozen. He'd never seen this coming. In the chaos he'd been dealing with since coming into work hours before, he'd never imagined finding himself in this predicament. Cedrick had pulled the wool over his eyes right from the start. All of the other inmates being freed were never meant to be anything more than a distraction. It was all a ruse so Cedrick could free one inmate in particular; the one who would do the most damage to the human world. Phillip couldn't think of anything more to say. There was only one thing to do now. Kill Cedrick. He looked toward the stake.

"Try again," said Cedrick. "Who knows, you might make it this time."

The vampire was unsteady on his feet, touching his burnt head gingerly and swaying in place. A boxer still recovering from a massive punch. Swelling with pride, he reveled in the knowledge that, after all these centuries, humans would finally pay for their treatment of his kind. Like any other creature, vampires had simply wanted their right to exist and to feed, but Van Helsing admirers like Phillip had never let them

Crag Island

be. One lonely day in his cell, Cedrick had come across the solution; vampires weren't capable of stopping humans on their own, so they needed to employ stronger allies.

Phillip lunged. Cedrick sidestepped. They both reached toward the stake on the floor at the same time, human ducking low, vampire reaching over him. Pain in Cedrick's eye intensified, and caused him to misjudge the distance to the stake. He reached out too far and hit the wall. By the time he realized his folly, he knew it was too late. A blur of motion passed his unburnt eye, and he turned toward it. Massive force drove him backward, and he had to backstep until he hit the office wall. The crash was loud and caused a lamp to fall on the opposite side of the room. The force was still there, pushing deeper into his core.

Driving the stake always forward, forward, forward, Phillip didn't dare let up. Cedrick would never allow him such an opportunity again. He stepped further toward his enemy, gripping his weapon first with two hands and then removing one to pound the back of it further into the creature's body. The stake stabbed in until only its base was exposed, the rest of it caked with the blood of the vampire's slowing heart.

Cedrick's mouth opened wide and then his face settled into an expression of serenity as he began to slide slowly to the floor. It had taken two hundred fifty-four years for death to find him, but here it was at last. He didn't mind any longer. His work was done. Eyes making contact with Phillip one final time, Cedrick grinned and watched as his hand crumbled to dust in front of him. Next, his arm began to flake away in pieces. He felt bits of his face peel away, then drop to the floor. A moment later, there was only dust where the vampire had stood before.

Phillip had to sit to catch his breath. Keeping constant pressure on the stake had been exhausting. He wanted nothing more than to sit in that chair and take a long rest, but he knew he couldn't. A minute or two was all he could spare and then he had to go see if it really was too late. Had Cedrick's plan succeeded? He was afraid he already knew the answer.

***

Forty-two minutes had passed with no sign of anyone roaming the corridors. Not since her near run-in with the mummy had Katarina felt the presence of any other being in the area. The never-ending anticipation of an encounter with an inmate was second only to the fear that came with the encounter itself. She wished she hadn't forgotten the knife in the far hallway, but didn't dare to go back.

The halls narrowed as she inched along, startled by every shadow, wincing at each sound. Window and door frames appeared smaller and she realized where she was. This was B Wing, the oldest part of the penitentiary. It had been mentioned in passing on her tour of the building a mere two days ago. She looked into each cell, grateful to find each one empty, while wondering where its occupant had gone.

She turned left down the corridor, then spied a puddle of water below a small broken window. She almost looked away, but stopped herself.

Ripples in the water.

There was no wind.

But there was a vibration.

It was low at first, then it grew louder, and the ripples in the water moved faster. She turned slowly.

It was huge, head almost touching the ceiling. The beast's eyes were small opal holes set above a long-twisted snout. It bared snarling meat-shredder teeth at her and bellowed with its bass voice, which echoed off the wall and reached her at a louder volume. The creature was covered in a mass of thick brown fur and crouched low, forepaws set on the floor, long black claws on display. A predator set to strike.

Katarina couldn't move. For the second time in the past hour, she found herself frozen by fear. She wasn't supposed to be here, patrolling the corridors, fighting the big bads. She was the failure, the one who hadn't passed basic training due to a repressed memory brought up to the surface of her mind by a flashing image: an old lady with white hair and bloody skin, reaching toward her from a large screen. Somewhere, deep inside her, a little girl had screamed and it had been her voice. She was supposed to be sitting at a desk, being annoyed by Will, while the real guards did the hard work. The beast growled with canine resonance and walked toward her on all fours. As it advanced, she saw its features clearly.

This is the king of wolves.

Suddenly, she knew. This was the one she should fear above all others. Here was inmate Eighty-four. This was Ivan.

The wolf raised his head and sent up a piercing howl that carried off all the walls and hit her with enough force to make her step back. It was the most terrifying sound she'd ever heard, but it also made her understand that she was capable of movement. This was no nightmare in which she was moving in slow motion while being pursued. She could run.

Katarina dashed away down the left corridor and took the next turn at full speed. She sprinted without consideration for anything other than gaining ground, putting as much space as possible between herself and the werewolf. She didn't need to look behind her to know it had followed.

Another turn came, then another. She was losing count of the corridors and had long since lost her sense of where she was in the prison. All that mattered was that the beast was closing the gap between them. She had to run faster, but her burning legs told her it couldn't be done. Ivan would catch up with her before long.

It took all her willpower to stop; only the knowledge that her legs would fail her if she continued made it possible. Flight no longer being an option, Katarina was left with a simple choice: Fight or die. She reminded herself that she hadn't failed every aspect of the obstacle course. When it was time to shoot, she'd hit every target they'd given her.

The werewolf came loping down the corridor, hairy arms planting themselves side by side on the hard floor, followed by great swinging hind legs that gave it a hunter's stride she could never hope to match. One bound of Ivan's equaled several of her steps and, seeing him move like this made her understand that it was only the twisting corridors that had allowed her to stay ahead this long. In a straightaway, she'd be doomed.

She drew her gun. Ivan roared, and the walls of the prison trembled. The vibrations made Katarina's hands shake as she positioned herself.

Only her training could save her now. She planted her feet shoulder-width apart, held her gun with two hands, and executed a precise Weaver stance. Ivan was closing. Closing.

Katarina drew in a breath and, against all of her instincts, stood still, waiting for her shot. One second later, it came.

Boom! The report of the gun bounded off of the walls, and hit her ears with the force of the wolf's howls. She shot again. Then paused, before firing a third bullet. Katarina had aimed well and knew it. All three bullets struck Ivan straight in the heart. Big as he was, he couldn't hope to withstand her marksmanship.

He wasn't stopping.

Impossible.

Three perfect shots, just as she'd been trained and Ivan wasn't even slowing down, didn't seem to acknowledge having been shot. And now he was dangerously close. The gun was of no use against him. There was no time to think. She didn't even have the chance to hope that her weary legs were still capable of getting her out of this. There was only the most primal urge every animal feels when death comes calling. Run!

Wind lashed at her back and she understood without looking that he'd swatted at her, barely missing. The chance she'd taken by trying to fight had cost her priceless distance. As she turned the next corner, hair coming undone from its braid, Katarina saw her greatest fear. This corridor was long and no adjoining halls were in evidence. She didn't see any place to turn. This was where she would die.

Windows rushed by; doors blurred in her peripheral vision. Her aching legs had not yet succumbed to the inevitability of death, and they ran on, ignoring the defeatist messages the mind was sending. She hurt more than she ever had in her life. Her lungs burned. In a moment, her legs would give out and she would collapse. Katarina hoped the end would come quickly.

A sign: EXIT.

The sign hung over a doorway. Beyond the doorway was a set of stairs. She could stay in the killing box of a corridor or try for the stairs. The choice was simple.

The wolf swung a massive claw at her again, but he missed as she sharply turned left, jumping through a red-rimmed door frame.

She was climbing steps, but wasn't far ahead. One leap would put him on top of her. Ivan charged. His left arm reached out, his right leg kicked. As he propelled himself forward, the great wolf found that he was unable to make progress. Every movement was strained in a battle against the restrictive doorway. After years in a cell, his wolf mind had forgotten how big he was in the small spaces of the prison. The ferocity that had enabled him to tear the throats of everyone from Londoners to Parisians was not enough to get through a B Wing door frame. He thrashed and pushed, but his right leg and arm remained in the tight confines of the doorway, unable to push through. Ivan was stuck.

Katarina stopped. Something had changed. She no longer heard the heavy canine pant of the hunter behind her. Instead, he whined. She turned. Ivan was still in the doorway, his body only halfway through the tight door frame. He groaned with effort, but could not force his huge body any further. Katarina laughed, despite herself. The fearsome inmate Eighty-four was being foiled by a doorway. She was grateful for the diminutive nature of B Wing.

Ivan stopped his thrashing and looked at her, dead in the eyes. The look told her what she needed to know; the beast was too determined to stop, his ravenous hunger far too powerful to be blocked by something as petty as a doorway. This was nothing but a setback. He would get through this door and when he did...

Katarina looked up the steps and saw that they connected to another flight not far above. That flight of steps led to a white door. Stenciled paint on the door read Roof Access.

A loud noise brought her attention back to her opponent. She couldn't see the source of the sound, but she could hear a short thump every few seconds. It was getting aggressively louder. The wall around the doorway was beginning to crack. He was going to smash his way through.

Katarina looked back at her exit. She could make it to the roof. Then what? The wolf would crash through the wall and find her up there. There would be nowhere for her to go once he did. The prison roof would be every bit as much of a trap as the hallway. If she was going to try something, it had to be now.

Once again, her mind went to the bone-handled knife that Phillip had made such a fuss over. Surely, it could've helped her here. Katarina forced the thought away. It was as useless as the gun. That knife might as well be miles away. She began searching her gear and her pockets, hoping to find a surprise weapon that had magically appeared for her, like Perseus with his singing sword and charmed helmet. But she was not Perseus. She was nothing but a rookie prison guard to whom the penitentiary gods had given an unhelpful gun, a lost knife, and…

The wall now featured a large crack, descending with each strike from Ivan's mighty hand. It wouldn't hold for much longer.

From her pants pocket, Katarina withdrew the strange bag of powder that Phillip had given her. The thought of the office made her long for the protection of the salt circle. None of this would've happened if she had taken Phillip's advice and stayed put.

What was the stuff in the bag?

After a second, it came to her.

AgNO3.

As the giant wolf progressed in bashing the wall around the tight doorway, Katarina questioned why Phillip had given her a small gray bag of powder in the first place. It must have a use, but what that could be eluded her. She took a deep breath, allowing herself a moment to think. This is what she knew: the chief of security had given her this powdered substance in a bag. He had also warned her specifically of inmate Eighty-four. Ivan was the only one Phillip had taken the initiative to mention. It followed that the powder could have something to do with Ivan. As the break in the wall grew steadily larger and Ivan eyed his would-be prey, Katarina considered the letters themselves: Ag seemed to go together as well as NO.

"Ag?" she spoke aloud. It helped her to process the thought and fight her growing fear. "Ag, I think, is a name for silver on the periodic table. And NO...maybe it's some kind of nitrogen/oxygen combo."

A large hole burst through the wall, and Ivan's second arm was now visible. He'd be coming at her any moment now. He roared with earth-shaking power.

There were stories of werewolves being killed by silver bullets. She remembered them from training two days before. Phillip had mentioned being out of bullets while they were in the office. What if she was correct? What if $AgNO_3$ was a mixture containing powdered silver? A part of her mind shouted that she was thinking along the wrong lines, wasting precious time, but that line of thought left her with no course of action, so she pushed it aside. If she was indeed holding the exact substance she needed, how could she use it against this hulking beast? It was no bullet.

A loud crash resonated through the stairwell, and she knew her time was up. Ready or not, Ivan was coming. Without further thought, Katarina stepped forward—one, two hesitant steps. The werewolf, shoving aside the last of the busted wall, was stepping out of the doorway. From only a few feet away, she could see how much he was salivating. He was hungry. One giant foot moved forward, and Katarina reached into the plastic bag.

This has to work, she told herself.

As the monstrous wolf advanced, Katarina raised her hand to her lips. She waited until Ivan was only a foot away, then leaned forward and blew into her hand. The powder flew in a gray cloud through the air, floating lightly, then settling on Ivan's snout, seeping into his eyes, and dropping into his open mouth. She stepped back and looked down. The bag was empty. Either this would work or she was dead where she stood.

The wolf howled again and took another step. Upon touching ground, his foot faltered as though he wasn't sure how to place it. Ivan reached a long-clawed hand toward her only to stop a moment later, staring at his fur. It was fading from his arm, flaking away like dried grass. Katarina beheld what might have been a wolf's expression of horror; eyes bulging, tongue lolling out, and his mouth opening widely as it emitted guttural noises.

He snapped at her, but stopped after a single try. It appeared to cause him pain to open his jaws so wide. Ivan scratched at his mouth, trying to root out something he could feel but not see. Blood seeped up and over his jowls, dripping down to the floor in front of him. Canine yips emanated from him as he sank slowly to his knees, claws incessantly seeking to tear the pain away. Katarina saw the wolf's eyes go a deep red a moment before sprays of blood began spurting out from behind them. He howled in the pitiable manner of a large puppy.

A softly spoken part of her wished she could save him, attempting to convince her that he was an innocent animal who'd done no more than follow his instincts, but she wouldn't have known what to do even if she could. It was a foolish thought, and she silently reprimanded herself for having it. Life for Ivan equaled death for her. It was that simple.

Lying sprawled out on the floor, the wolf was no longer great. He had shrunken. A Great Dane with a massive coat of fur. He convulsed on the floor as large tufts of his fur scraped off on the ground. The blood hadn't stopped trickling from his eye sockets. Katarina looked away. She couldn't bear the sight of his suffering. Turning did not block the sounds, which were worse. The bag of silver nitrate, she now understood what this weapon was, was still clutched in her hand. She tossed it on the floor, left it empty, took one long deep breath, and turned back around.

The wolf was gone. In its place lie a man. Curled on the floor, he was of middling height. His hair was tousled sepia running down a thin neck on a body of too-white skin. He looked sickly, as though he'd been drained of blood. It occurred to Katarina that that wasn't far from what had truly happened.

She stepped closer and beheld the twitching man below her. His blue eyes were open wide and stared vacantly at the wall he'd recently smashed to pieces. Once again, she discovered a well of pity within herself for an inmate. Unlike Fergal, Ivan had surely committed violent crimes, resulting in peoples' deaths. There was no way to know how much of the blame to place on the beast or the proper amount to set on the human, but none of it mattered any longer. The creature he'd been for so long was now extinct and only this pale being remained, broken and fading. Katarina knelt next to his shaking body and placed a gentle hand on his shoulder.

"Ivan?" she said.

The vacant eyes shifted position and found her. They were pale circles of Arctic light. A slight smile showed the edge of his mouth.

"*Kahk tee-byah zah-voot?*"

"What?" she asked.

Ivan lifted a shaking hand and pointed to himself, speaking, "Ivan." Then he pointed to her and repeated his question.

"Katarina," she answered.

His smile grew larger as his arm descended. Ivan's last word was "*Krasivaya.*" Katarina, whose grasp of Russian didn't extend beyond 'Da', walked away from his fallen body, never to learn that after countless years of feeling nothing but animal aggression, Ivan had looked into her eyes and declared her, "Beautiful."

Leaving B Wing behind, Katarina made her way to the far side of the prison. It wasn't long before she was supposed to meet Phillip back in the security office. She looked forward to it. The endless winding hallways and white walls were unsettling. Anything could be around the next corner. Knowing that the gun was now her only weapon didn't help at all.

She pressed on, twisting and turning through the corridors. Things around her were becoming more familiar and she knew she wasn't far now. Maximum Security was behind her, only the last stretch to the security office remained. Despite her best efforts, Katarina's hopes of arriving without incident began to rise.

"There she is."

The voice came from her left and Katarina made an abrupt turn toward it. A figure emerged from the shadows, and she found herself staring into eyes as dead and empty as a shark's. A snaggle-toothed face, weathered by time, stared back at her. Margaret Harrow came into full view and reached out toward her.

"You ran off," accused the witch. "Ahh, but now, your little man is not here to get in the way."

Katarina found herself unable to move once again. It was the same as before, paralysis born of fear. The witch moved closer. There was, however, something different about this encounter with Margaret. As a gnarled old hand reached out toward her, Katarina understood that it was she, herself, that had changed. The Katarina of fifty-six minutes ago had been nothing more than a rookie prison guard. She had become Officer Anderson, Killer of the Wolf King. Such a woman would not allow Margaret Harrow to have her way.

"Not only a coward, but a stupid girl as well," cackled Margaret. "See what you left behind." The old hag raised her hand to show the long mysterious knife Phillip had given Katarina in the office. As her old fingers tightened on the bone handle, the witch smiled and said, "You had exactly what you needed, and you lost it, child. Clearly, you don't deserve to wield it. This weapon could have saved you an awful lot of trouble."

Hand reaching down to her hip, knees bent in preparation for action, Katarina stood fast. She raised her gun to eye level. The bewildered look in the old hag's eyes fortified her. Fear cracked apart and made way for defiance. Margaret opened her mouth wide and was about to speak when Katarina pulled the trigger.

Click.

"Stupid girl," laughed the witch, her cackle growing louder each second as Katarina stared at the useless gun. "Now your bones are mine." Margaret reached out her long sharp fingers.

Katarina silently berated herself for forgetting to reload. She was a rookie and was acting like one. But as the witch's hand drew closer and the knife remained clenched in the hag's other hand, the young woman realized something about herself that Margaret didn't understand. She was more angry than frightened.

Knocking Margaret's arm aside, Katarina stepped forward and slammed her knee into the witch's gut. For all her magic, the witch couldn't defend herself against such physical aggression. She was nothing but an old brittle lady, bent and wheezing, as a much younger stronger woman pried the knife from her hand. When Margaret was able to stand again, she found herself looking at the waiting Katarina, the bone-handled knife held en-guarde in her right hand.

"Your bloody parents were supposed to give you to me decades ago!" shouted Margaret Harrow. "Now you stand here threatening me? Foolish girl. You belong to me! You always have."

The memory flashed through her mind again; she was a child, an old woman smeared blood on her. Had it been…no…

"It was you. You were the old woman painting me with blood," said Katarina, her eyes widening.

"Yes," said Margaret. "It's about time you figured it out. Your mommy and daddy made a deal. They gave you to me. Then they took you back. I was in the middle of my ritual. Your youth would have made me beautiful again, but they interrupted me. They went back on the deal!"

"What did you give them?" asked Katarina.

"Gold. Sapphires, rubies, diamonds. It's all they cared for. Only wealth."

"I don't believe you," said Katarina.

"Why do you think you're here, child? You came to work in this horrid place because I marked you long ago. You're mine and you always have been!"

Katarina drove the long knife into Margaret's stomach, twisting the blade, shoving with all her might until the old hag's body went limp and fell to the ground.

Katarina grabbed the knife, pulled it slowly from the body, and held it up to eye level. Soaked in blood, bits of inner organs slid off the blade. Such a simple thing, nothing but a bit of bone and metal, and not a particularly well-preserved object, but it apparently held power that she'd never had the opportunity to understand. She would be sure never to misplace it again.

Walking away from the dead witch, she hoped that someday she would find the answers to what happened to her long ago. Did her parents really give her away to a witch? Why would they do such a thing?

She reached the office and stepped inside the circle of salt, with minutes to spare. With a long sigh, Katarina flopped against the desk she'd bumped into earlier. Had it only been one hour?

As she observed the space around her, something ran through the back of her mind. She couldn't pinpoint it, but something was off. It ate away at her.

"Katarina!"

Phillip rushed in as though he had something important to tell her. He was bruised with cuts on his arms and face. He stepped into the office.

"It was him," said Phillip. "Cedrick. I know what he's done. It's even worse than I thought."

Phillip told her about his encounter with the vampire as he fought to control his exasperated breathing. Katarina was miles away, focused only on the floor, and the terrifying observation she had made.

"Are you listening?" asked Phillip. "This is extremely important."

Katarina took her eyes away from the floor and looked at Phillip. He awaited her answer with a furrowed brow and crossed arms.

"Phillip," she said. "Look, the circle!"

It took a second for the significance of her words to reach him. Phillip looked to what had caught her attention. The large salt circle that gave the security office its magical protective barrier was incomplete. On the edge nearest the door, a small streak of salt had been wiped away, nullifying the circle's power, and taking away their only safe haven in this place. He looked back up at Katarina.

"Who...?"

It was all he could say before a hand came in through the doorway and grabbed him by the neck. He tried to pull back away from the mummy, but it was too late, the damage had already been done.

His mouth stretched to an impossible length as his hands rose to his face, all the while skin began to dry and pale; Edvard Munch's 'The Scream' made real. Phillip fell to his knees as hairs on his arms slipped off his rapidly drying body. The mummy stood by his side the entire time, one hand resting on his cheek. Through the thick wrappings, Katarina thought she saw a skeletal smile.

Staring at the dry cracked shape that had been her security chief seconds before, Katarina wondered how this had happened. The circle had been breached, allowing the intruder entrance. It meant that someone with magical capabilities had understood the circle's power well enough to break its connected energy. Once imbued with the will of its creator, the power of the salt circle was said to be a solid defense from most of the creatures in the penitentiary. It had failed for the first time in its existence, and Katarina thought she knew why.

Margaret Harrow had been near here.

The witch was exactly the kind of inmate that would be able to undermine such a magical defense. Even in death, she was dangerous. If only Katarina had killed her sooner.

The mummy looked at her. It was done with Phillip, having drained all the life it could from him, but it wanted more.

Katarina jumped backward, against the opened window leading out into the hall. Daring to turn her back to the mummy, she jumped out.

Running again, she chanced a look behind her. The mummy was far behind and wasn't following. She slowed to a walk.

Phillip was dead. She couldn't believe what she had seen. He had dried up like a body left in the baking sun, and then flaked away piece by piece, all in a manner of seconds. Unlike Fergal and Ivan, Phillip had been one of her own.

Katarina fought to gain control of her thoughts again. This wasn't over, and she was now the only security in a position to do anything about it.

As she pressed on down the corridor, she felt cold settling in, seeping through her clothes, into her skin, and creeping down into her bones. Rain struck the hallway at an angle, through what once had been the east wall and now was crumbling brick.

Outside, beyond the hole, massive waves were crashing against the island rocks. Wind thrashed at the outer walls, tossing broken branches and various debris into the penitentiary. A storm was brewing and sought to invade the prison interior. Katarina stood, watching, and wondered how this could be possible.

Before Phillip's last moment...She couldn't go there. It was too fresh in her memory, so Katarina skipped the thought. She chose to think only about what Phillip said and not what had occurred afterward.

"Inmate One-Hundred-One."

Phillip had mentioned it a moment before she'd interrupted him with her warning about the broken circle. Now, as she stood staring outside as rain slashed her face, Katarina struggled to recall what she'd heard. There had been something about size. Phillip had gestured with his hands spread out wide, indicating an enormous creature. Phillip's gesture hadn't come close to illustrating the immensity of One-Hundred-One.

As she stepped out into the early morning storm, Katarina looked at the sky. Gray clouds were darkening as they rolled in one after the other, relentlessly pressing down. Crag Island was being assaulted by both sky and sea. Shivering in the cold, watching the waves crashing on the rocks below, Katarina tried to find solace in the thought that whatever/whoever the inmate was, it would still be trapped on the island.

"...planned perfectly...the only one who could...enormous casualties..."

Snippets of Phillip's last words ran through her mind. While she'd been distracted by the broken circle, he'd been trying to impart the full impact of Cedrick's plan to her. The vampire had never been planning his own escape. The mass breakout had been nothing more than a cover for a more sinister goal. All along, Cedrick had only wanted to release one inmate: the one who could do the most damage to the species he hated most.

Katarina felt the darkness encroaching as amorphous beasts of nimbus roiled far above her head. One person couldn't hope to quell the uprising in the prison alone, so she did the only intelligent thing that came to mind and launched a flare high into the dark sky, hoping it would be seen by a passing ship. Water splashed her, and she knew it wasn't the rain this time, but a wave seeking her up on the high ground. The sea was rising, the clouds descending, set to the task of swallowing Crag Island whole. She tried the walkie she'd nabbed from an office on the way out, tuned it to the mainland frequency, and got nothing but a garbled reply. If she had no communication with the mainland, there was no help coming, and there was no way of letting them know what had happened. As she pondered this and shivered for reasons that had nothing to do with the cold she felt, Katarina remembered one more thing. On Sunday, a guard had been talking about the biggest inmate in the prison; a great beast more ferocious than he'd ever seen in his ten years working at the facility. She thought back to what he'd told her and fixed on one thing that worried her more than the creature's size. He'd said it clearly, and Katarina did not doubt her memory.

"Inmate One-Hundred-One has wings."

The End

Crag Island

Printed in the USA
CPSIA information can be obtained
at www.ICGtesting.com
CBHW011512250624
10644CB00012B/133